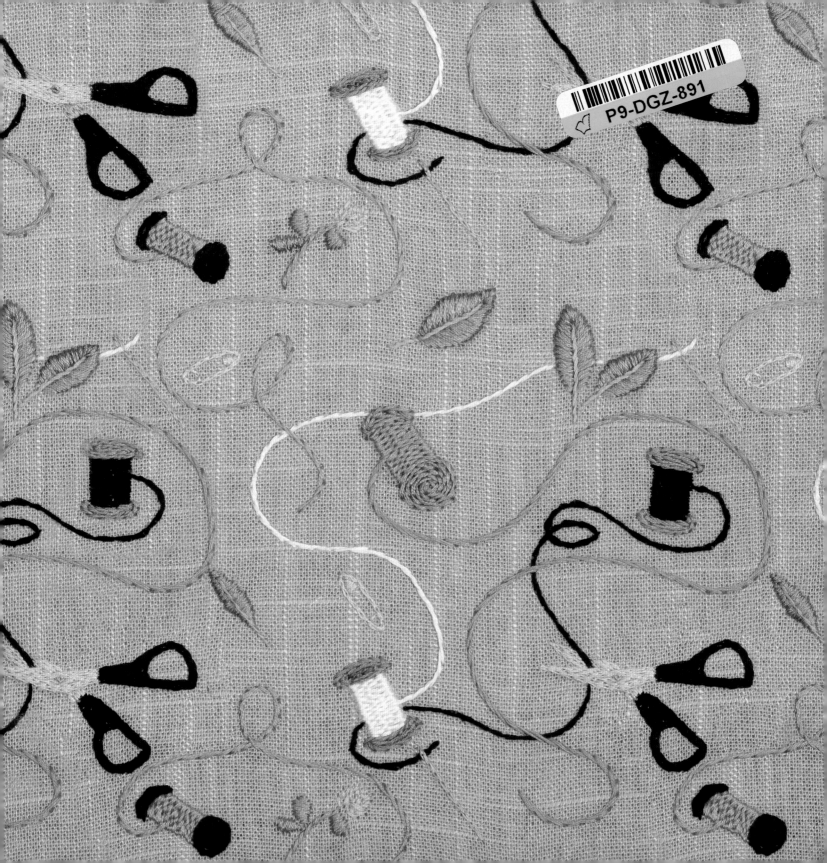

For my parents, who always encouraged my creativity;
for Joe, who keeps me from losing my head like Mr. Buttonman;
and for Ellie, who inspires me daily.

Joelle

Published in 2019 by Simply Read Books
WWW.SIMPLYREADBOOKS.COM
Text & illustrations © 2019 Joelle Gebhardt

LIBRARY AND ARCHIVES CANADA CATALOGUING IN PUBLICATION

Gebhardt, Joelle, author, illustrator
     Mr. Buttonman and the great escape / written and illustrated by Joelle Gebhardt.

ISBN 978-1-77229-028-8 (hardcover)

     I. Stories without words. I. Title. II. Title: Mister Buttonman and the great escape.

PS8613.E29M73 2019   jC813'.6   C2018-903501-3

We gratefully acknowledge for their financial support of our publishing program the Canada Council for the Arts, the BC Arts Council, and the Government of Canada.

Manufactured in Malaysia

Book design by Joelle Gebhardt & Heather Lohnes

10 9 8 7 6 5 4 3 2 1

Mr. Buttonman
and the Great Escape

Joelle Gebhardt

SIMPLY READ BOOKS

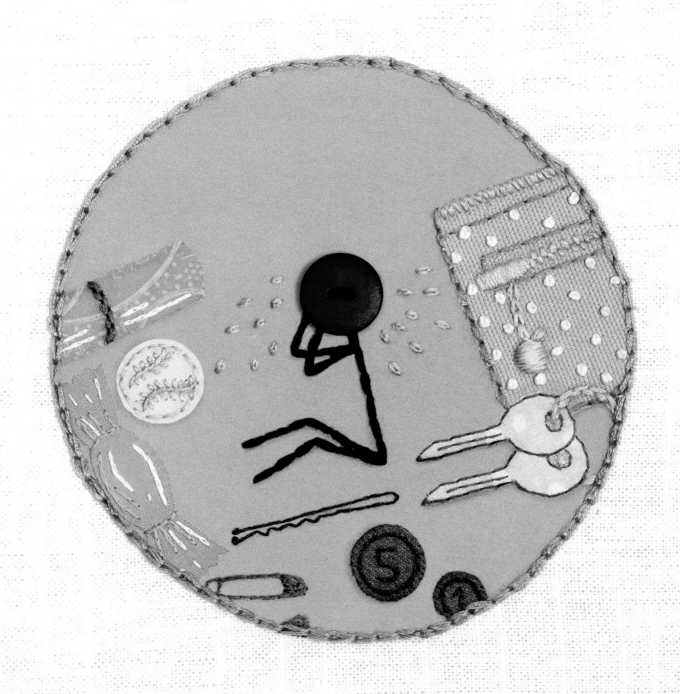

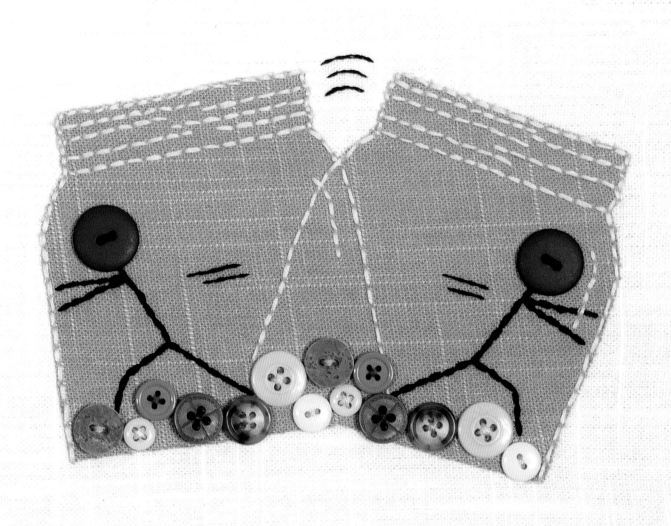

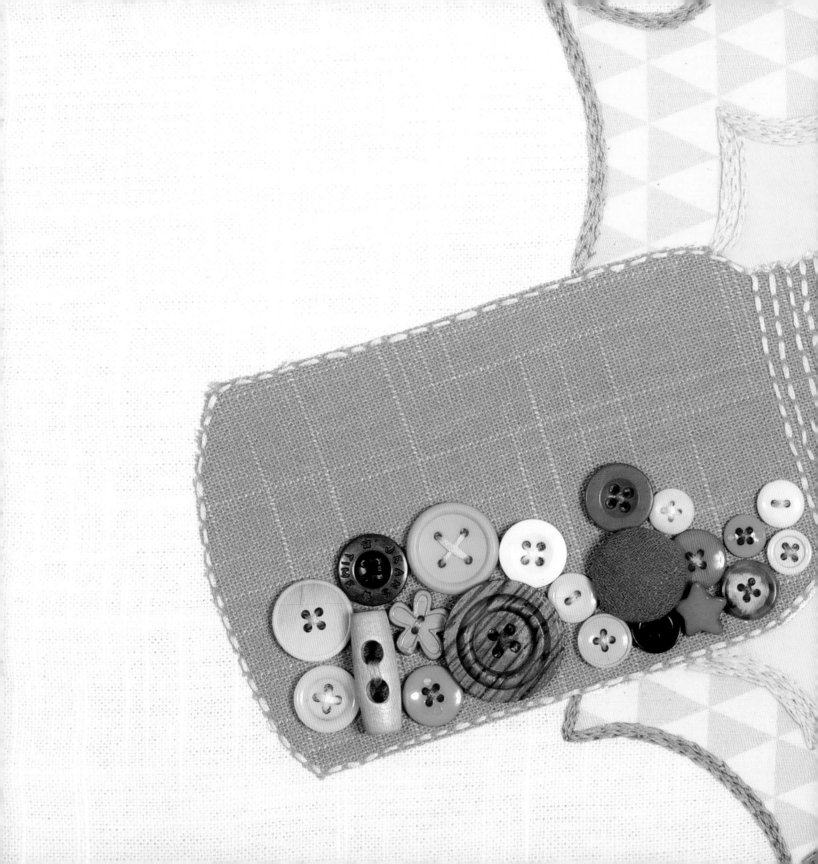

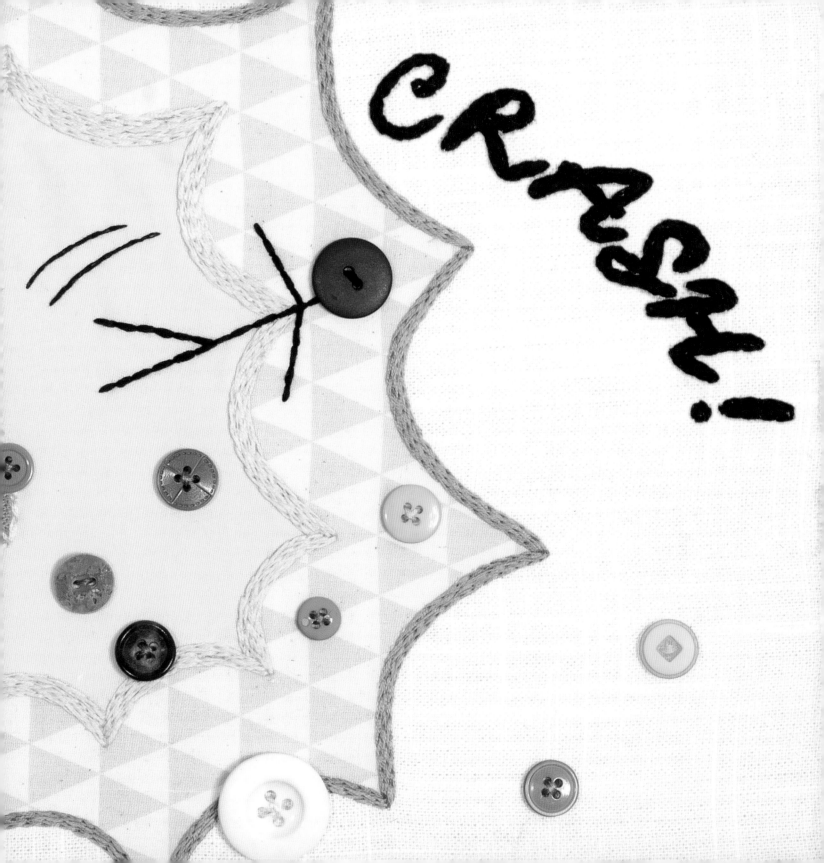

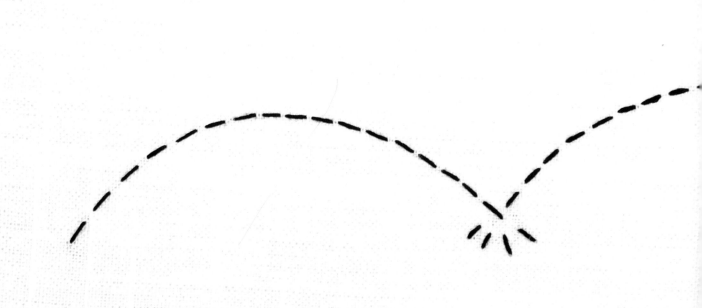

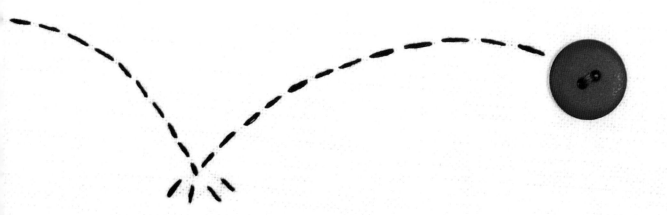

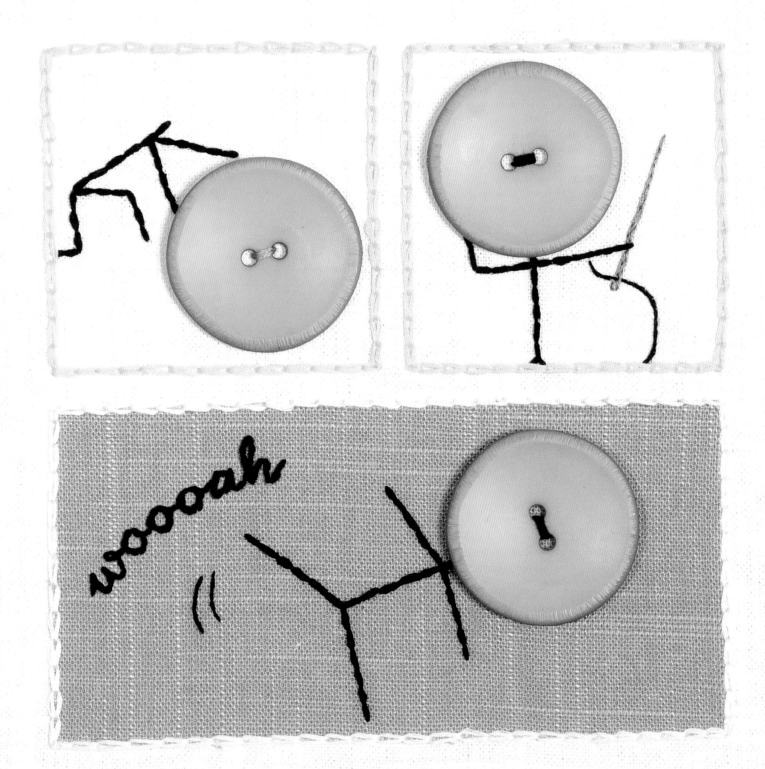

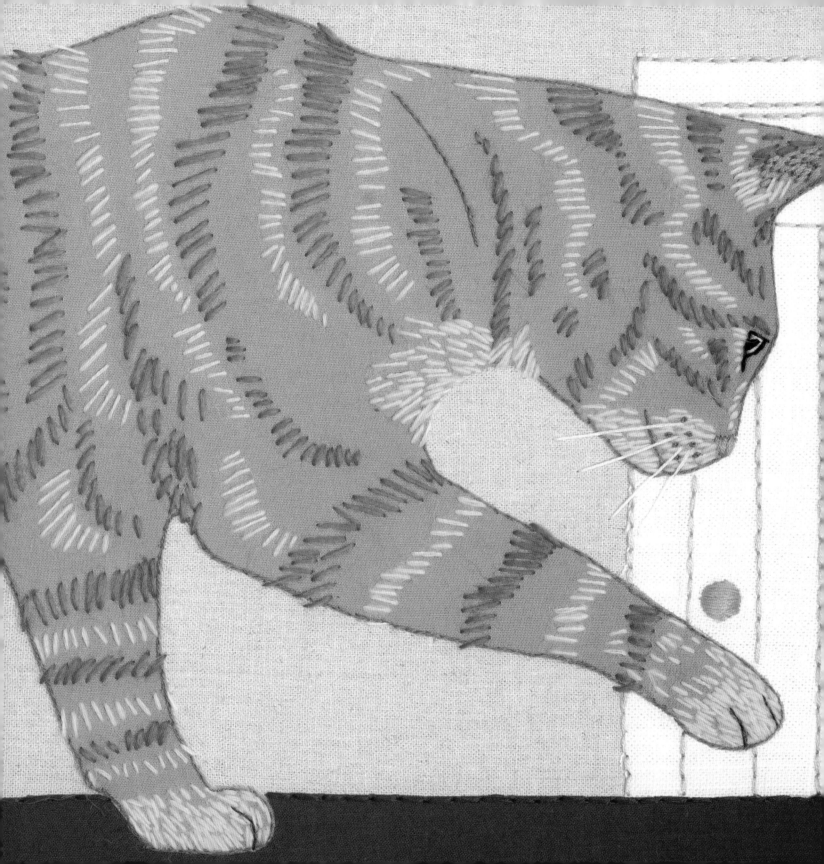

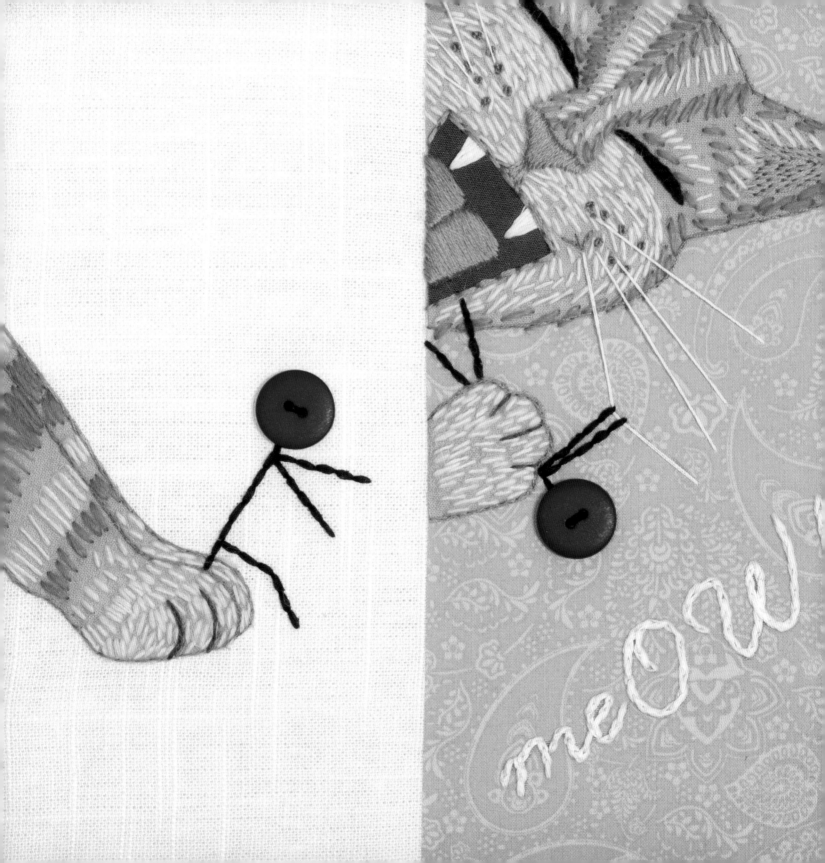

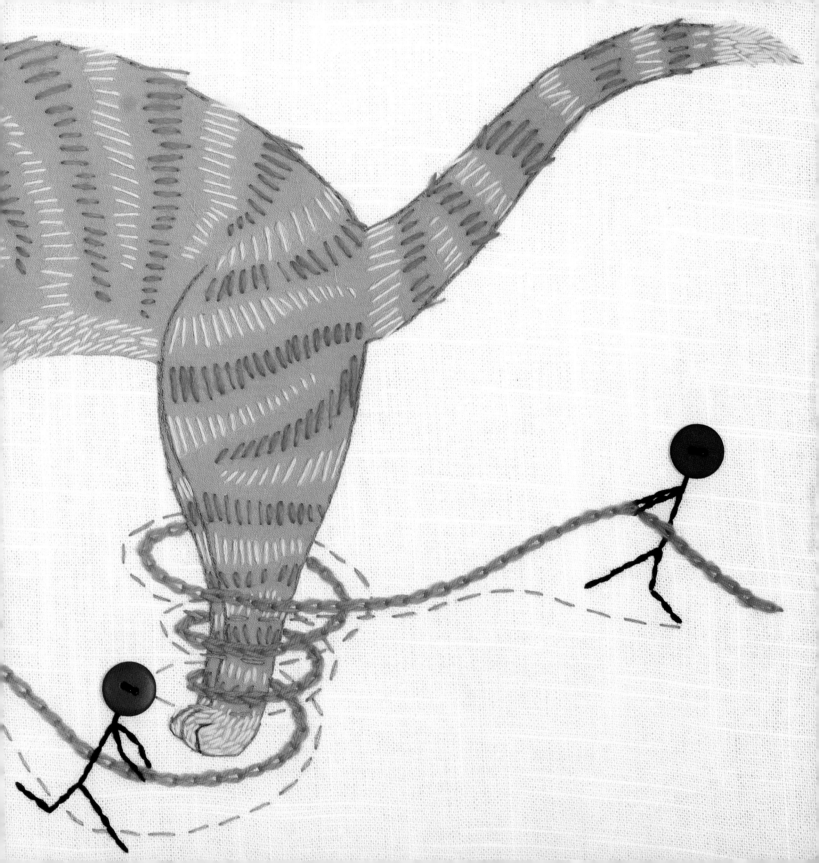